There Are Seven Homes on My Street

A Child's View of Religions

By Ron Flowers and Anise Flowers

AuthorHouse™
1663 Liberty Drive
Bloomington, IN 47403
www.authorhouse.com
Phone: 1-800-839-8640

Published by AuthorHouse 10/10/2014

ISBN: 978-1-4969-3834-3 (sc)
ISBN: 978-1-4969-4798-7 (hc)
ISBN: 978-1-4969-3835-0 (e)

authorHOUSE®

In memory of April,
the "Mama Flower,"
and her love of children.

Hi,

My name is Ron.

And I want to tell you about the 7 houses on my street.
There are many different types of people on my block.
Some of them can even speak a different language.
And all of them have a different view of God.

My father isn't sure if there is an outside god who created us all or not.

He thinks we could be natural happenings because the Universe is so large.

My dad says we are just one of billions and billions of star systems and that there may be other people out there on other planets.

People who are uncertain about God are called agnostics. My Dad works as a scientist and scientists usually believe in things that they can see or test in some way. But, there are other things, like God, and life after death, that cannot be proven and will always be unknowable.

My dad told me that it doesn't bother him to be uncertain about God. He likes a good mystery story, and these questions are just more mysteries. My dad feels that the mysteries in life keep things exciting.

I asked my dad why there are so many religions in the world.
He said that in all places around the world,
even in olden times, people wanted to know why they were
here. They wanted to connect with the source of everything
because they felt so small and the Universe seemed so large.

People were also afraid of death and wanted to know if
they would continue on in some way after they died.
All of the religions around the world give answers to these
questions. I asked which religion is right, and my dad
told me I should decide for myself. So I have been
talking to the other children on my street to learn more
about their religions.

My friend Mark lives up the street and he is a Christian. His family goes to church every Sunday.

He told me God made the first person out of dirt, which reminded me of a potter I saw last summer at a theme park.

The potter made different shaped pots out of clay and then he set them out to dry. The pots looked so lovely sitting there, all in a row.

Mark said all of the animals and fish were also created by God, but that God loves us best of all.

In Sunday school, Mark learned the story of Jesus who died on a cross to save all of us. God created everything; then people got into trouble and did bad things. And so God sent Jesus, who was his son, to die for us, so that the bad things would be forgiven and everyone could go to Heaven.

If you believe in Jesus, then you can go to a wonderful place called Heaven after you die and live there forever.

Mark's living room has some pretty crosses on the wall and his Mom wears a cross necklace. I think the cross is an important symbol for Christians about Jesus and their faith.

For Christians, God is like a father, only a lot bigger because God can see everything and know everything, all around the world.

I spent the night at Mark's house once and I noticed that his family prays to God to bless their food before they eat. Also, Mark's parents taught him to pray to God each night. Mark prays about people he loves or prays for things he wants to have in his life. Mark believes that God has a plan for each person and we have to accept God's will for us.

Mark's church gave him a Bible that tells about God, and it has Mark's name printed in gold letters on the front. On the inside, everything that Jesus says is printed in red ink and Mark thinks that is really cool.

Emily and her little sister live across the street from me.
Her parents are Taoist. I didn't know what that meant.
They may be calling God by another name. Emily said
this thing called Tao didn't create the universe, but rather,
gave birth to it, like a mother gives birth to a baby. In Taosim,
everything in the universe, including us, is like babies which
grow like flowers, from the inside out.

Tao is in everything and in everyone.

One day I asked Emily if this thing called Tao was not created by an outside force, then where did everything come from?

She told me the Universe created itself by dividing things up into pairs of opposites. Things like hot and cold, up and down, good and bad, or life and death seem quite different. But they are really just two sides of the same coin. Everything is known because it has an opposite.

This is the symbol that the Taoists use to show the opposites together.

I thought it looked like two fish playing together. In Taoism, everything is like this symbol. No matter how different things look on the outside, they are all connected on the inside, and everything is really one thing.

One day there was a fire in Emily's house.
The fire trucks came and put it out.

I think the fire was Emily's fault but I was surprised that her
parents didn't seem to get mad or upset.
Later, I asked her why they weren't mad and she told me that
nothing bothers her parents. Emily's parents taught her to
always accept what happpens and to go with the flow.
Those who follow the Tao flow as if they are like water and
always try to follow the path of least resistance.

The stangest idea came from Isham, the oldest kid on the block. His family are all Hindus.

Isham said God is like an actor who plays all of the different parts, like in a play.

Isham said we are all God on the inside.
But we have forgotten who we are and so we are lost playing our different roles.

The joy of life is seeing that you are what God is doing.

I learned that Hinduism is the oldest religion and has no founder or single teacher. They see God, called Brahman, in many different forms which are just God wearing different masks.

When Brahman takes the form of individual people he is called Atman.

I asked Isham why Brahman created the world and he said that Brahman did not have a reason. Life is just for the fun of it, like when you play baseball.

I like the idea that for Brahman, all of the world is a playground.

I asked Isham what he thought would happen when he died. According to his parents, he will come back again in a new life. I wondered if this continues forever, but Hindus believe that eventually you learn everything you need to know and then you can rest for awhile.

There is a girl who I like on my block named Sophia.
The other kids say her parents are Muslim.
But Sophia told me her parents are really Sufis.

Sufis are the mystical part of the church and they are known for their dancing. They spin and spin like tops and this spinning brings them closer to Allah.

Allah is what they call God. Allah so wanted to be loved and known, that he broke himself up into millions of pieces and created the Universe out of himself.

Sophia thinks maybe Allah was just lonely
and wanted company.

One day I was talking with Sophia about a pirate movie
I had seen where they were looking for buried treasure.

Sophia told me that in their bible, which is called the Koran,
it says Allah is like a hidden treasure and he wants to share it
with all of us.

This hidden treasure is inside of us.

So, life is like a big treasure hunt to find God within yourself.

In order to find this treasure, Sophia and her family pray
several times a day, chant, and meditate on Allah's love.

I wondered whether Sufis would go to Heaven like the Christians when they die. Sophia said of course they would, but you don't have to wait until you die to know Allah. By doing good deeds and your daily practices, you can become close to God now, while you are still alive.

Sophia can write God's name in Arabic.

The word means making peace and obeying God's will. There are laws that man makes, and there are spritual laws that God makes.

Since all of life is a journey to God, you must try to follow all of these laws if you want to be with God.

Alex is my best friend and he lives next door. His parents are Buddhists and they have no God. Alex said they meditate a lot which changes your feelings about being separate from the world. With meditation, you feel at one with everything around you.

Buddhists believe that feeling at one with everything makes you happier and makes everything around you prettier. If you believe you are separate from the world, you will desire things and this will make you unhappy since you can't have everything you desire.

I learned from Alex that they called themselves Buddhist because that was the name given to the first teacher.

Buddha means "The one who woke up." Alex said we spend so much time talking to ourselves inside of our heads that we don't see the world as it really is.

Life is kind of like we are asleep and dreaming.

Buddha wanted everyone to wake up as he did.
So Buddha taught that if you stop all the talking to yourself by meditating, then you can wake up.
With this new awareness, you will know better who you are and what is really going on around you.

Buddha told his followers not to take other people's word for things like God or heaven, or to believe the things they read in books. Buddha thought people should quiet their minds so that they could experience these truths for themselves.

Talking to Alex, I started thinking that Buddhists are a lot like the Hindus because they also believe we will be reborn again and again. Only we don't remember our past lives.

Buddhists call this the wheel of life because we go round and round in endless cycles.

Karma means that how you live this life determines how your next life will turn out. Good deeds create good Karma and bad deeds create bad Karma.

When you have gone around long enough,
you become enlightened.
Being enlightened frees you from the wheel.
Then you feel perfectly happy,
no matter what is going on around you.

The only child in the last house on my block is a little baby girl. Her mom, Carol, is very nice and talks to me like I'm a grown-up. Carol said she will teach her daughter that God is everywhere and is inside of all the children in the world. She believes each of us can feel our oneness with God.

I was surprised because Carol said how you think impacts how you feel and how you live your life. Apparently, whatever you focus on in your life will expand. So if you give your attention to happy things, then more happy experiences will come. Like if I pay attention to my spider plant, then it grows and there are more spider babies. But if I don't pay attention and take care of it, then my plant will not grow.

Carol and her baby often sit on one of the benches in the park
next door and watch me and my friends play.
They seem very happy.

Carol told me that happiness is a matter of keeping a positive
attitude and knowing that all is well with the world.
One should listen to the small voice that lives
inside your heart.
By following your inner voice,
you can connect directly with God.

All people are responsible for connecting to their inner spirit
and for creating their own lives.

Carol told me that she stays happy by paying attention to her thoughts and feelings. When she is feeling bad, she looks for thoughts that will take her back to a happier feeling.
If you can look at things in a different way, you can feel better.

She used the story of the Ugly Duckling as an example.
The duckling thought he was ugly until he found out he had grown into a swan. So it was the way he thought about himself that made him happy or not.

The more we love each other, then the more we become spiritual beings, just like the duck changed into a swan.

I asked if she thought we go to heaven when we die. Carol said we have always been eternal and we will always be eternal.
Since God is within all of us, heaven is also inside of us, all the time. We create our own heaven through our beliefs, our feelings, and our connection to our inner spirit.

Sometimes after school all of the kids on my street meet at the park. Everyone gets along really well and we all have fun playing together. Thinking about all these different ways of looking at God, I can't help wondering if maybe they are all true. Maybe each religion is just a different way of looking at the same thing. Maybe it's just how close you look, like when you see through a microscope or a telescope. Anyway, the differences don't seem to matter to the kids on my street.

How is it on your street?

Ron Flowers and Anise Flowers are a father and daughter writing team. Ron is extremely well-read in world religions and scientific theories. He is a retired scientist and long-time follower of Eastern religions. Ron primarily describes himself as a Buddhist. He has written two previous books available at free-ebooks. net. *What Is?*, co-written with his brother Steve Flowers, is a dialogue between Christianity and Eastern religious philosophies. The second book, *Fingers Pointing, Birds Singing* is a compilation of spiritual quotes. Ron has lived in Mountain Home, AR for thirty-five years and currently resides there with his two dogs, Midge and Caramel.

Anise Flowers, Ph.D. is a Clinical Child Psychologist. After being raised by a Christian mother and a Buddhist father, Anise has always had an interest in the beliefs of different religions. She has been writing puppet shows for eight years which teach children and adults about metaphysics and New Thought. Her puppet shows are regularly performed at Creative Life Spiritual Center in Spring, Texas. Anise lives in The Woodlands, TX with her son, Tucker, and two Labrador retrievers. For more of her writings on motherhood, spirituality, and Psychology visit her blog at *aniseheartjoy.com*.

CPSIA information can be obtained
at www.ICGtesting.com
Printed in the USA
BVHW050533160819
555925BV00011B/64/P

9 781496 938343